Jim Henson's

SPLASH AND BUBBLES™

The Greatest Treasure of All

Based on the series created by John Tartaglia
Based on the TV series teleplay written by Michael Foulke
Adaptation by Liza Charlesworth

Houghton Mifflin Harcourt
Boston   New York

Download FREE music from Splash and Bubbles!

Download two tracks from
Splash and Bubbles: Rhythm of the Reef
(Songs from Season One)
by visiting **www.splashandbubblesmusic.com**
and entering the code: SPLASHMUSIC

Available for a limited time only.

ISBN: 978-1-328-97346-7 paper over board
ISBN: 978-1-328-97345-0 paperback

hmhco.com

Printed in China
SCP 10 9 8 7 6 5 4 3 2 1
4500728529

It was a great day for a treasure hunt! Splash, Bubbles, Dunk, and Ripple found lots to add to their collections. "I can't decide which is my favorite," said Ripple. "This shell, that shell, or the other shell!"

Flo the sea turtle was impressed.

"I had no idea you were such amazing treasure hunters," she said. "I know of an even bigger treasure, if you kids are interested."

They were!

Flo told them the treasure was hidden in an artificial reef.

"What's an *artificial* reef?" asked Bubbles.

"Sometimes things from above sink down to the ocean floor," Flo said. "Over time, plants and animals move in and a reef is born!"

"Wow! How do we find it?" asked Splash.

"How about a treasure hunt?" asked Flo, and she gave them their first clue. *"You want to find a treasure, and you may get your wish. Start in Reeftown, where a playful fish is not a fish.* Good luck!" said Flo, swimming away.

The clue was tricky. Finally, Splash figured it out.
"A dolphin is playful, and is a fish that isn't a fish,
because dolphins are mammals!" he shouted.

That's it! The next clue must be waiting at Dolphin Canyon. They didn't spot any dolphins there. But they did see their oyster pal, Pearlene!

"Hey, everybody," she said. "What brings you to Dolphin Canyon?
It's not like I have any . . . *clue* . . . what you're doing here."
Pearlene giggled.

Pearlene gave them their next clue:

*"Your treasure's not far, not a long way to go.
Your next clue can be found in the cleanest place you know."*

Hmm. What was the cleanest place they knew?

"The kelp forest is pretty clean," said Ripple.

"It's not *pretty* clean!" said Splash. "Tidy keeps it *really* clean. That's gotta be it!"

At the kelp forest, they found
Tidy cleaning up, as usual.

Sure enough, he had another clue:

"When you leave the forest, you'll be closer than it seems,
when you see the top of a rock that shines and gleams.
The treasure you seek is big, not small.
And inside it, you'll find the greatest treasure of all."

The kids thought and thought. The top of a rock
that shines and gleams? What could that mean?
But the clue also said they were close!

They swam out of the kelp forest. They hadn't gone very far when they found a shiny rock! This must be the place, but Tidy's clue said the treasure was big . . .

When they turned around, they couldn't believe their eyes!

The artificial reef!

"It's beautiful!" Bubbles said.

"Come on, guys," said Splash. "This is a reef and we're Reeftown Rangers. Let's do what we do best . . . explore!"

FIN FACT:
Any manmade object that sinks to the ocean floor can become an artificial reef. They can be sunken ships, collapsed bridges, even lighthouses!

Flo had said that the real treasure would be hidden inside the artificial reef. But where?

Dunk peeked inside a dark cave. It was cool!
But he didn't find any treasure.

"This thing spins!" said Bubbles.
It was interesting, but it wasn't treasure.

"Did *you* find any treasure?" Bubbles asked Splash hopefully.
"Nah, just some shiny stuff," said Splash.

Where, oh where was the treasure?

Suddenly, Ripple announced, "I found it!"

"What? Where?" asked the others.

Ripple smiled at her friends. "We'll never run out of games to play in this artificial reef, but the greatest treasure of all is having endless fun with each other," she said.

Just then, Flo swam up.

"I knew you would find the artificial reef," she said with a grin.

"But you kids even managed to figure out the greatest treasure of all."

FIN FACT:
Sometimes scientists build artificial reefs to replace damaged natural reefs, so the sea creatures will still have a great place to call home.

"I hereby declare this artificial reef the official clubhouse of the Reeftown Rangers!" said Splash.

Splash, Bubbles, Ripple, and Dunk loved playing together in the Reeftown Rangers Clubhouse. They were happier than if they'd found all the treasure in the sea.

"Ocean friends forever!" they cheered.